BABY SHARK
Doo Doo Doo Doo Doo Doo

BEBÉ TIBURÓN
Duu Duu Duu Duu Duu Duu

Art by / Arte de
John John Bajet

Scholastic Inc.

Watch out for a dance guide at the end of the story!

¡No te pierdas la guía del baile al final del libro!

Originally published in English as *Baby Shark Doo Doo Doo Doo Doo Doo*

Translated by Abel Berriz

Copyright © 2018 by Scholastic Inc.
Translation copyright © 2020 by Scholastic Inc.
Adapted from the song, "Baby Shark."

ISBN 978-1-338-60112-1

10 9 8 7 6 5 4 3 2 1   20 21 22 23 24

Printed in the U.S.A.   40
First Spanish printing, 2020
Designed by Doan Buu

A long, long time ago, there lived a . . .

Hace mucho, mucho tiempo, había un...

Baby Shark, doo doo doo doo doo doo.
Baby Shark, doo doo doo doo doo doo.

Bebé Tiburón, duu duu duu duu duu duu.
Bebé Tiburón, duu duu duu duu duu duu.

Baby Shark, doo doo doo doo doo doo.
BABY SHARK!

Bebé Tiburón, duu duu duu duu duu duu.
¡BEBÉ TIBURÓN!

Mama Shark, doo doo doo doo doo doo.
Mama Shark, doo doo doo doo doo doo.
Mamá Tiburón, duu duu duu duu duu duu.
Mamá Tiburón, duu duu duu duu duu duu.

Mama Shark, doo doo doo doo doo doo.

MAMA SHARK!

Mamá Tiburón, duu duu duu duu duu duu.

¡MAMÁ TIBURÓN!

Daddy Shark, doo doo doo doo doo doo.
Daddy Shark, doo doo doo doo doo doo.
Papá Tiburón, duu duu duu duu duu duu.
Papá Tiburón, duu duu duu duu duu duu.

Daddy Shark, doo doo doo doo doo doo.
DADDY SHARK!
Papá Tiburón, duu duu duu duu duu duu.
¡PAPÁ TIBURÓN!

Great White Shark, doo doo doo doo doo doo.
Great White Shark, doo doo doo doo doo doo.
Great White Shark, doo doo doo doo doo doo.

Gran Tiburón Blanco, duu duu duu duu duu duu.
Gran Tiburón Blanco, duu duu duu duu duu duu.
Gran Tiburón Blanco, duu duu duu duu duu duu.

GREAT WHITE SHARK!
¡GRAN TIBURÓN BLANCO!

Grandma Shark, doo doo doo doo doo doo.
Grandma Shark, doo doo doo doo doo doo.

Abuela Tiburón, duu duu duu duu duu duu.
Abuela Tiburón, duu duu duu duu duu duu.

Here they come! Doo doo doo doo doo doo.
Here they come! Doo doo doo doo doo doo doo.
¡Aquí vienen! Duu duu duu duu duu duu.
¡Aquí vienen! Duu duu duu duu duu duu duu.

Here they come! Doo doo doo doo doo doo.
HERE THEY COME!
¡Aquí vienen! Duu duu duu duu duu duu.
¡AQUÍ VIENEN!

Shark attack! Doo doo doo doo doo doo.
Shark attack! Doo doo doo doo doo doo.
¡Ataque de tiburón! Duu duu duu duu duu duu.
¡Ataque de tiburón! Duu duu duu duu duu duu.

Shark attack! Doo doo doo doo doo doo.

SHARK ATTACK!

¡Ataque de tiburón! Duu duu duu duu duu duu.

¡ATAQUE DE TIBURÓN!

Swim real fast! Doo doo doo doo doo doo.
Swim real fast! Doo doo doo doo doo doo.
¡Nada de prisa! Duu duu duu duu duu duu.
¡Nada de prisa! Duu duu duu duu duu duu.

Swim real fast! Doo doo doo doo doo doo.
SWIM REAL FAST!
¡Nada de prisa! Duu duu duu duu duu duu.
¡NADA DE PRISA!

Safe and sound! Doo doo doo doo doo doo.
Safe and sound! Doo doo doo doo doo doo.
¡Sanos y salvos! Duu duu duu duu duu duu.
¡Sanos y salvos! Duu duu duu duu duu duu.

That's the end! Doo doo doo doo doo doo.
That's the end! Doo doo doo doo doo doo.
That's the end! Doo doo doo doo doo doo.
¡Este es el fin! Duu duu duu duu duu duu.
¡Este es el fin! Duu duu duu duu duu duu.
¡Este es el fin! Duu duu duu duu duu duu.

BABY SHARK DANCE! ♫ ¡EL BAILE DE BEBÉ TIBURÓN!

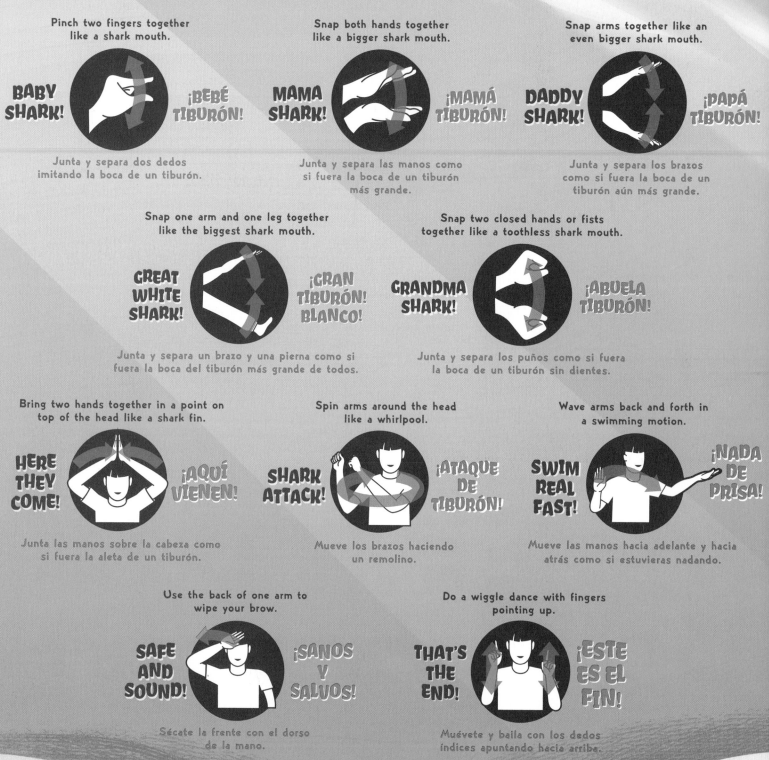

Pinch two fingers together like a shark mouth.

BABY SHARK! **¡BEBÉ TIBURÓN!**

Junta y separa dos dedos imitando la boca de un tiburón.

Snap both hands together like a bigger shark mouth.

MAMA SHARK! **¡MAMÁ TIBURÓN!**

Junta y separa las manos como si fuera la boca de un tiburón más grande.

Snap arms together like an even bigger shark mouth.

DADDY SHARK! **¡PAPÁ TIBURÓN!**

Junta y separa los brazos como si fuera la boca de un tiburón aún más grande.

Snap one arm and one leg together like the biggest shark mouth.

GREAT WHITE SHARK! **¡GRAN TIBURÓN! BLANCO!**

Junta y separa un brazo y una pierna como si fuera la boca del tiburón más grande de todos.

Snap two closed hands or fists together like a toothless shark mouth.

GRANDMA SHARK! **¡ABUELA TIBURÓN!**

Junta y separa los puños como si fuera la boca de un tiburón sin dientes.

Bring two hands together in a point on top of the head like a shark fin.

HERE THEY COME! **¡AQUÍ VIENEN!**

Junta las manos sobre la cabeza como si fuera la aleta de un tiburón.

Spin arms around the head like a whirlpool.

SHARK ATTACK! **¡ATAQUE DE TIBURÓN!**

Mueve los brazos haciendo un remolino.

Wave arms back and forth in a swimming motion.

SWIM REAL FAST! **¡NADA DE PRISA!**

Mueve las manos hacia adelante y hacia atrás como si estuvieras nadando.

Use the back of one arm to wipe your brow.

SAFE AND SOUND! **¡SANOS Y SALVOS!**

Sécate la frente con el dorso de la mano.

Do a wiggle dance with fingers pointing up.

THAT'S THE END! **¡ESTE ES EL FIN!**

Muévete y baila con los dedos índices apuntando hacia arriba.